Hair & Make-up

Philippa Wingate and Felicity Everett

Edited by Philippa Wingate
Illustrated by Kathy Ward and Conny Jude
Designed by Kathy Ward and Camilla Luff

Consultants: Sally Norton and Saskia Sarginson
Photography by Howard Allman and Ray Moller
Series editor: Jane Chisholm
Series designer: Amanda Barlow

With thanks to Non Figg and Ruth King

Contents

Purchased with
Neighbourhood Renewal
Fund money

Make-up

CONTENTS

ALL ABOUT MAKE-UP

Make-up is exciting and colourful. You can wear as much or as little as you like. The most important thing is to wear make-up that suits you and is right for the occasion.

YOUR MAKE-UP KIT

Before you begin to experiment with make-up, you need to collect a basic kit. From lip brushes to cosmetic sponges, this section of the book will tell you exactly what you need. There's also advice on which shades of eye-shadow, lipstick and blusher will flatter your colouring.

Find out what these brushes are used for on page 9.

SKIN CARE

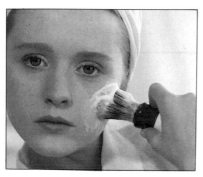

This section of the book will show you how to test your skin to find out whether it is dry, greasy or normal.

A really effective daily cleansing routine is crucial for healthy skin, so there is advice about which products you should use and how to give your skin a special deep cleansing treatment.

APPLYING MAKE-UP

It is essential to apply your make-up properly. The techniques included in this section of the book are described step-by-step so you know exactly what to do.

As well as a basic natural make-up and a glamorous evening look, there are some colourful and original ideas for really spectacular party make-up.

A COMPLETE BEAUTY TREATMENT

While taking trouble with your face, you shouldn't neglect the rest of your body. The useful top-to-toe beauty treatment described on pages 20 to 23 includes cleansing and moisturising your skin, a manicure for your hands and feet, and recipes for face masks that contain a variety of natural ingredients.

LOOKING AFTER YOUR SKIN

It is important to look after your skin properly, especially if you wear make-up. You should cleanse and moisturise it every day.

This picture shows you what you will need.

Tissues and cotton balls are useful for taking off make-up and for putting on creams and lotions.

Toner is liquid which closes up the pores after you have cleansed your skin.

Cleanser is cream or lotion which you use to clean your skin and take off your make-up.

Eye make-up remover comes in liquid or pads. It removes make-up from the sensitive skin around your eyes.

Cotton buds are good for touching your face without making it dirty.

Moisturiser is cream or lotion which protects and softens your skin, and stops it from becoming too dry.

Cotton wool balls

Cleansing brush to use with cleansing bar

Cleansing bars are good to use instead of cleanser if your skin is oily.

DIET

For clear, healthy skin, eat plenty of fresh fruit and vegetables and drink lots of water. Avoid eating sweets.

PROBLEM SKIN

If you often get rashes, use "hypoallergenic products". They are less likely to irritate your skin than ordinary products.

SPOTS

If you get spots, use medicated skin products. If you have a bad one, dab it with a cotton bud soaked in lemon juice.

WHAT SKIN TYPE ARE YOU?

Look for skin care products recommended for your type of skin. To test your skin type, press a piece of sticky tape lightly over the bridge of your nose and on to your cheeks. Avoid the area around your eyes.
Pull it off and examine it.

White flakes = dry skin
Drops of moisture = oily skin
Both = normal skin

DRY SKIN

Can cause flaky patches. Skin may feel "tight" after washing.

OILY SKIN

Often looks slightly shiny. Tends to be spotty.

NORMAL SKIN
Dry in parts and oily in others. Also called combination skin.

CLEANSING

Follow this simple cleansing routine every morning and evening.

1. To remove you eye make-up, dab make-up remover around your eyes with cotton wool or use ready-to-use pads. Make sure that you don't pull the skin around your eyes, as it is very delicate and sensitive.

2. If you use a cleansing bar, lather your face with a shaving brush, then rinse it off. Alternatively, you can smooth cream cleanser over your face and neck, then wipe it off with a tissue.

FINDING THE RIGHT PRODUCTS FOR YOUR SKIN

This chart shows you which creams and lotions suit different types of skin.

To find out what type of skin you have, do the simple test on page 5.

SKIN TYPE	CLEANSER	TONER	MOISTURISER
Dry skin	*Cream cleanser*	Mild toner: rose water, camomile or still mineral water	*Cream moisturiser*
Oily skin	*Lotion, cleansing milk or a cleansing bar*	Natural astringent, such as witch hazel or cucumber	*Light, non-greasy liquid moisturiser*
Combination skin	*Cream cleanser*	Mild toner: rose water, camomile or still mineral water	*Thin cream or thick lotion*

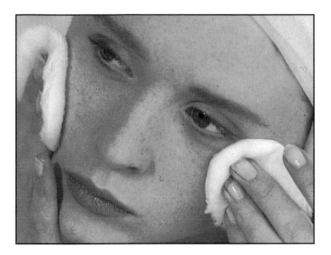

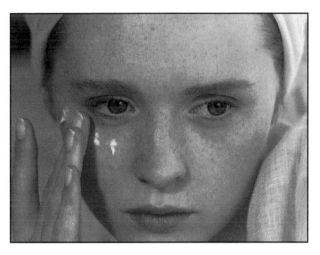

3. Soak a cotton wool pad in toner and wipe it over your face. Alternatively, you can put the toner into a spray bottle. Dab your face dry with a paper tissue to remove the excess toner.

4. Put little dots of moisturiser over your face and neck, and gently rub it into your skin with the tips of your fingers. If necessary, you can put more on drier areas, such as your cheeks.

DEEP CLEANSING

Deep cleansing about once a fortnight helps to keep your skin soft and really clean. Any of the methods shown below work well.

Facial scrubs – These contain tiny granules which rub off the top layer of your skin. Read the instructions on the packet for what to do.

Facial sauna – Hold your face about 20cm above a bowl of steaming hot water. Drape a towel over your head to stop steam from escaping. Wait for five minutes.

Face masks – You can buy gels, creams, or mud-based masks. Choose one which suits your type of skin. Read the instructions on the packet for what to do.

YOUR MAKE-UP KIT

On these pages you'll find everything you need to do a complete make-up, like the one shown on pages 16-19.

Pencil sharpener

Eyelash curlers

Sponge-tipped applicators

CONCEALER

Concealer is a cover-up cream which hides spots and blemishes. Choose one a bit lighter than your skin colour.

FOUNDATION

Foundation is a creamy liquid which gives your skin an even colour and texture. It comes in different shades.

FACE POWDER

Face powder stops your skin from looking shiny. A natural colour called translucent is usually best.

BLUSHER

Blusher comes as powder or cream. It adds colour to your face. You can also use it to shape your face (see page 13).

EYE PENCILS

Eye pencil is for outlining your eyes, close to your eyelashes. Choose a shade darker than your eye-shadow.

EYE-SHADOW

Eye-shadows come in different forms: pressed powder; in pots of powder or cream; or in pencils of

powder or cream. To start with, buy a set of two matching pressed powder eye-shadows.

MASCARA

Mascara is a brush-on liquid for darkening your eyelashes. Black or brown is best for everyday use.

Tissues

Cotton wool
balls

Eyeliner brush

Eye-shadow brush

Cosmetic
sponges

Lip brush

Blusher
brush

Powder
brush

Powder puff

LIPSTICK

Lipstick adds colour and
moisture to your lips. To put
it on properly, you need a
lip pencil and a lip brush.

LIP GLOSS

Lip gloss can be worn over
lipstick, or on its own. It
makes your lips look shiny
and stops them from chapping.

Eyelash and
brow comb

An old toothbrush
works just as well
as an eyelash and
brow comb.

CHOOSING COLOURS

It is fun trying out make-up colours, but mistakes can be expensive. It's best to choose shades which suit your colouring.

Here are six typical hair and skin colours. Beside each picture, you can see the make-up colours which flatter that type.

FAIR SKIN AND BROWN HAIR

Brunettes often have quite fair skin and rosy cheeks. If your skin looks blotchy sometimes, try using a creamy-beige foundation to even out the tone.

LIPS

Pale pink *Coral* *Rich red*

EYES

Blue *Apricot* *Grass green* *Gold* *Sand brown*

CHEEKS

Tawny pink *Golden peach*

FAIR SKIN AND BLONDE HAIR

Blondes have fair skin, which has a tendency to be rather dry. It needs careful skin care. Try using a pinkish foundation to add some colour to your skin.

LIPS

Sugar pink *Peach brown* *Warm pink*

EYES

Grey *Soft brown* *Cornflower blue* *Violet* *Pinky mauve*

CHEEKS

Beige pink *Peach*

FRECKLED SKIN AND RED HAIR

Redheads tend to have fair, freckled skin. It is usually quite sensitive. Make sure you choose a light foundation which lets your freckles show through.

LIPS

Pale peach *Burgundy* *Raspberry*

EYES

Rust *Tawny pink* *Golden brown* *Plum* *Sage green*

CHEEKS

Amber *Dusky pink*

Several companies make foundations and concealers especially for dark skin. Mix two colours together if you can't find the right shade. Don't wear powder. It makes your skin look dull. Let a natural sheen show through a light coating of foundation.

BLACK SKIN AND DARK HAIR

Black skin can be quite oily, and sometimes the colour is a little uneven. It is a good idea to even out the tone by using a light, non-greasy foundation.

LIPS

Shocking pink   *Pillar box red*   *Wine red*

EYES

Golden brown
Navy blue
Rose
Buttercup
Orange

CHEEKS

Burgundy
Brick red

OLIVE SKIN AND DARK HAIR

In winter, olive skin can sometimes look rather sallow and it may be oily. A non-greasy, dark beige foundation can make it look healthy and golden again.

LIPS

Copper   *Chestnut*   *Burgundy*

EYES

Pink beige
French navy
Plum
Moss green
Gold

CHEEKS

Burgundy
Copper

BROWN SKIN AND DARK HAIR

Brown skin has a tendency to be slightly blotchy. Mix foundation and concealer, and then use the mixture all over your face to even out your colouring.

LIPS

Shocking pink   *Oyster pink*   *Brick red*

EYES

Tawny gold
Mauve
Plum
Yellow
Blue

CHEEKS

Mauve
Golden brown

SHAPING AND SHADING

On these pages you can find out how to use shader, highlighter and blusher to make the shape of your face look more oval, and to show off your best features.

It is a good idea only to wear shader and highlighter when you go out in the evenings. They can look too obvious during the day.

HIGHLIGHTER

Highlighter is light-coloured powder you use to show off your best features. A light shade of eye-shadow will do instead.

SHADER

Shader is pinky brown powder you use to make your face look slimmer. A dark shade of blusher will do instead.

WHAT IS BEST FOR YOU?

Where you apply shader, highlighter and blusher depends on your face's shape. A quick and easy method of determining the shape of your face is described on page 38.

Once you have decided what shape your face is, take a look at the key. You can find out exactly where to put your highlighter, shader and blusher.

When you apply these, make sure you blend them in well, so that no hard edges show.

KEY:

///// *Shader*   WW *Highlighter*   ▮ *Blusher*

LONG FACE   SQUARE FACE   HEART-SHAPED FACE   ROUND FACE

SHADER

To make your cheekbones look higher, suck in your cheeks, and dot shader in the hollows below them. Blend it in towards your hairline.

To make your nose look slimmer, dot shader down each side of it, or wherever your nose is uneven. Blend it in with your fingertips.

To disguise a double-chin, dab shader beneath your chin and blend it in around your jawline. Make sure it doesn't look like a dirty mark.

HIGHLIGHTER

To highlight high cheekbones, dot highlighter just above your cheekbones and blend it in evenly, so it slants up towards your hairline.

To draw attention to your eyes, dab highlighter on to each browbone (the area just beneath your eyebrows) and blend it in.

Emphasize the shape of your mouth by using a lip brush to stroke highlighter into the dimple above your top lip. Then blend it in.

BLUSHER

To give your face shape and colour, brush blusher on to your cheekbones. Blend it in so that no hard lines show.

To give your face a hint of colour, dot blusher on to each earlobe. Then blend it in with your brush.

If you are looking pale, dab blusher around your hairline. Then blend it in thoroughly so that it is barely there.

THE NATURAL LOOK

All you need for a natural-looking make-up are the things shown below.

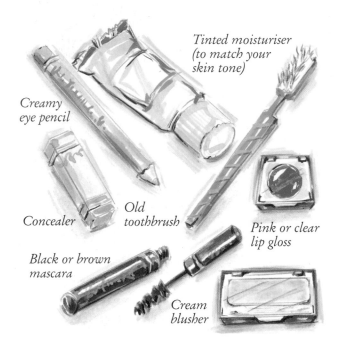

Creamy eye pencil

Tinted moisturiser (to match your skin tone)

Concealer

Old toothbrush

Black or brown mascara

Pink or clear lip gloss

Cream blusher

CONCEALER AND MOISTURISER

1. Tie your hair back. Wash your face and pat it dry. Dot moisturiser on with your finger and smooth it in. Cover any blemishes with concealer (see page 16).

BLUSHER

2. Use your fingertips to dot blusher on to your cheeks. Then carefully smooth the blusher outwards and upwards towards your hairline.

EYE PENCIL

3. Carefully draw a pencil line across your eyelid, next to your eyelashes. Smooth the colour over your eyelid, using a damp cotton bud or your fingertip.

MASCARA

4. Brush mascara on to your upper lashes, as described on page 18. Let it dry, and then apply a second coat. Brush one coat of mascara on to your lower lashes.

BRUSHING YOUR EYEBROWS

5. Use an old toothbrush or an eyebrow brush to brush your eyebrows upwards. Then wet your finger and smooth it over each eyebrow in the direction it grows.

LIP GLOSS

6. Using a lip brush, paint lip gloss carefully on to your lips. Do not brush it right to the edge of your mouth, as it can run and look rather messy.

THE FINISHED LOOK

7. This is what the finished natural look make-up should look like. With a bit of practise, you will be able to do it in a matter of minutes.

PUTTING ON YOUR MAKE-UP

1. Put your make-up on in a room with a mirror and lots of light. Tie your hair back. Wash your face and put on some moisturiser.

2. Dot a little concealer over any spots, blemishes or dark shadows, and blend it in well with the tip of your finger.

3. Dot a little foundation over your face. Put it over your lips too, but not on your eyelids, as it will make them oily.

4. Wet your cosmetic sponge, wring it out and blot it on a piece of tissue. Use it to spread the foundation evenly over your face.

5. Dip a ball of cotton wool into your tub of loose powder. Then pat the cotton wool firmly, but gently, all over your face until it is evenly covered.

6. Using a large, soft powder brush, flick any spare powder off your face. Brush it downwards to make the tiny hairs on your face lie flat.

If you get too much powder blusher on your brush, blow on it to remove some.

7. If a stubborn spot still shows through the foundation and powder, dab a clean brush on your concealer and paint it out.

8. Stroke your blusher brush across your powder blusher until it is lightly but evenly coated with powder.

9. Brush the blusher on to your cheekbones (this is the area just above your cheeks), and right up to your hairline.

10. Keep adding more blusher until the colour is strong enough. If it begins to look too obvious, you can tone down the effect with powder.

PUTTING ON YOUR MAKE-UP (CONTINUED)

For advice on selecting a shade of eye-shadow, see page 10 and 11.

11. Start by stroking the lighter shade of eye-shadow over your eyelids. Blend it in with a brush or sponge-tipped applicator.

12. Stroke the darker shade of eye-shadow on to the outer half of your eyelids. Blend in the edges with another brush.

13. Draw a fine pencil line along your eyelids, next to your lashes. Smudge the line slightly with a damp cotton bud.

14. Draw another line underneath your eyes, close to your lower lashes, as shown here. Smudge it gently, as before.

15. Carefully clamp the eyelash curlers around your top lashes. Hold them shut for a minute and then open them again.

16. Hold a mirror at chin level to brush mascara on to your top lashes. Look straight in to the mirror to do your bottom lashes.

Choose a lip pencil that is a similar shade to the lipstick you want to wear.

Using a lip brush will help your lipstick stay on longer.

17. Draw an outline around the edge of your mouth with a lip pencil, resting your little finger on your chin to steady your hand.

18. Coat your lip brush with colour from your lipstick. Carefully paint the colour on to your lips, keeping within the outline.

19. Blot your lipstick on a tissue, taking care not to smudge it. Then put on a second coat and blot your lips again.

20. To give your lips some shine, dot lip gloss in the centre of your lips and carefully brush it out towards the edges.

TOP-TO-TOE BEAUTY

Why not invite over some friends
and give yourselves luxurious
all-over beauty treatments.
Here is a step-by-step guide to
what to do.

STEP ONE: HAVE A BATH

1. Run a warm bath, adding some
moisturising bath oil or bubble bath.
Don't spend longer than 20 minutes
soaking, or your skin will start to wrinkle.

2. While you are in the bath take a handful
of coarse sea salt and rub it over your
bottom and thighs to stimulate your
circulation and make you tingle.

3. Massage your skin with a
textured bath mitt to rub
off any dead skin and leave
your body feeling smooth.

4. Pat yourself dry with a
towel. Dust some talc over
your feet and use deodorant
under your arms.

5. Massage moisturising lotion
all over your body. Pay special
attention to dry skin on your
heels and elbows.

STEP TWO: CONDITION YOUR HAIR

1. To make sure your hair
looks shiny and healthy,
follow the instructions on
page 44 to give it a special
warm oil treatment.

2. When you have applied
the warm oil, wrap
clingfilm around your hair.
This will prevent any oil
dripping onto your clothes.

3. Wrap a towel around your
head, and leave the oil
conditioning your hair while
you get on with your top-to-
toe beauty treatment.

STEP THREE: PUT ON A FACE MASK

While your hair conditioner is still working, put on a face mask. Read the instructions on the packet for what to do. Don't put the face mask on the skin just beneath your eyes, as this is very sensitive skin. You will find recipes for home-made masks below.

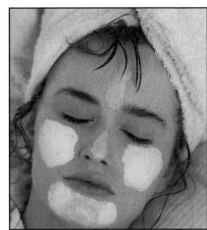

You can place thin slices of cucumber or potato over your eyes if you like. The slices are cool and will soothe your eyes.

Put on some relaxing music, lie back and rest for 10 to 15 minutes.

Finally rinse off the face mask with warm water and pat your face dry gently with a soft towel.

HOME-MADE FACE MASKS

For dry skin: mix together a teaspoon of runny honey and a mashed, ripe avocado. Spread the mixture on your face and leave the mask on for 15 minutes.

For oily skin: mix together a tablespoon of plain yogurt, a teaspoon of honey, a teaspoon of oatmeal and a mashed peach. Leave the mask on your face for 15 minutes.

For normal skin: peel and crush some cucumber to a pulp. Mix it with a teaspoon of plain yogurt and a few drops of rose-water. Leave the mask on for 15 minutes.

STEP FOUR: REMOVE UNWANTED HAIR

Everyone has hair on their legs. There is no need to remove it unless you want to.

If you do remove the hair on your legs, you must do it regularly. The hairs that grow back look thicker, because they are short and stubby.

Depilatory cream is the gentlest and easiest method of removing hair.

Read the instructions on the packet before you start. Spread the cream thickly over your legs with the spatula provided.

Leave it on for as long as the packet tells you. Then wipe it off gently with a wet cloth. Rinse your legs and pat them dry with a towel.

TOP-TO-TOE BEAUTY (CONTINUED)

STEP FIVE: A MANICURE

1. Treat your hands to a manicure before you go out. First, file your nails with an emery board. It is best to file from the edges towards the centre of your nails.

2. Soak your fingertips in warm, soapy water for a few minutes. If your nails are dirty, scrub them with a nailbrush. Dry your hands, and rub on some hand cream.

3. Rub some cuticle cream into the hard pads of skin at the base of your nails to soften them. Gently push back the cuticle with a cotton bud.

4. Paint on a thin coat of nail varnish. When it is dry, carefully put on another coat. There are some ideas for party nails on page 25.

STEP SIX: A PEDICURE

1. Now you can give yourself a pedicure. Trim your toenails straight across with nail clippers or scissors. Then file from the edges towards the centre of your nails.

2. Soften your cuticles with some cream and push them back gently with a cotton bud. Then separate your toes with cotton wool and put on two coats of nail varnish.

STEP SEVEN: RINSE YOUR HAIR

1. When your conditioning hair oil has been on for 30 minutes, wash it off. Shampoo your hair twice and rinse well.

2. Comb your freshly-washed hair through gently with a wide-toothed comb (see page 49).

3. If you have time, allow your hair to try naturally. Alternatively dry it following the advice on pages 50 and 51.

STEP EIGHT: STYLE YOUR HAIR

If you arc going out to a party or somewhere special, give your hair extra body and bounce using hair rollers. Follow the instructions on pages 52 and 53 to create corkscrew curls or soft waves.

When you take the rollers out, gently brush your hair, or just run your fingers through it, to separate the curls. You could use a little hairspray to hold the curl in your hair all evening.

STEP NINE: FINAL TOUCHES

1. Tidy up your eyebrows by plucking any hairs that grow beneath them. Pull them in the direction they grow.

2. Now put a little moisturiser on your face and do your make-up. See pages 24-31 for some ideas for party make-up.

3. Dab a little toilet water or perfume behind your ears and on the inside of your wrists and elbows.

PARTY MAKE-UP

Party make-up can be anything from bright lipstick, turquoise mascara, glitter and sequins to false eyelashes. On these pages you will see some useful things to collect.

Face and body glitter gel

Sequins and stars

Glitter dust

Coloured mascara

EYE-SHADOWS

You can buy sparkling powder eye-shadow in lots of colours. To stop it from spilling on to your cheeks, put it on with a damp brush.

MASCARA

You can buy mascara in lots of colours, such as green and violet. For just a hint of colour, brush it on to the tips of your lashes only.

EYEBROWS

Try colouring your eyebrows to match your mascara. Dab a little mascara on your eyebrow brush. Then brush your eyebrows with it.

PUTTING ON FALSE EYELASHES

1. Put these on before your eye-shadow. Apply a coat of mascara, then dot eyelash glue along the lash band with a pin. Make sure you glue each end.

2. Let the glue dry for a second. Then pick up the lashes with a pair of tweezers and position them on your closed eyelid, on top of your real lashes.

3. Gently press the lash band down on to your eyelid with your finger. Wait for the glue to dry, then brush the eyelashes upwards with an old toothbrush.

Brightly coloured nail varnish

FINGERNAILS

There are lots of amazing nail varnishes. Try using two colours at once, or stick on nail transfers. Make sure each coat is dry before you apply the next.

Lots of shimmery eye-shadows

Bronzing pearls to give you a healthy looking suntan

Lipsticks

False eyelashes

Eye pencils

GLITTER DUST AND SEQUINS

You can make shimmery lip gloss by mixing some glitter dust with your ordinary lip gloss in the palm of your hand. Brush it on to your lips with a lip brush.

Add shine to your make-up by gluing sequins on to your face with eyelash glue. Put them at the outer corners of your eyes, or glue one on your cheek as a beauty spot.

POLKA DOT MAKE-UP

This party make-up combines stylish black and white with fun polka dots for a stunning effect.

YOU WILL NEED:

- Light beige foundation
- Translucent powder
- White and dark grey powder eye-shadows
- Black eye pencil
- Black mascara
- Pale pink or white lipstick
- Matching lip pencil

For a more dramatic effect, use a foundation a shade lighter than natural tone.

1. First smooth foundation all over your face and neck evenly using a cosmetic sponge. You can check how to do this on page 16.

2. Apply translucent powder to your face fairly thickly using a cotton wool ball or a powder puff. Flick off any spare powder with a powder brush.

3. Brush a thick layer of white eye-shadow over the whole of your eyelid. If necessary apply a second coat to get a heavy, matt effect.

4. Brush dark grey eye-shadow along the line of your eye socket as shown. Broaden the line towards the outer corner of your eye and then blend it in with a brush.

5. Carefully draw a fine black pencil line along your eyelid, close to your upper eyelashes. Smudge it slightly with a damp cotton bud or your finger.

Take great care not to injure your eye.

6. Draw pencil dots on your eyelids. Press firmly but gently, turning the tip of the pencil slightly, so that the dots show up well.

7. Curl your eyelashes with your eyelash curler. Then brush two coats of mascara on to your upper lashes and lower lashes.

8. Brush your eyebrows into a neat shape with your eyebrow brush. Smooth a little Vaseline over your eyebrows to make them shine.

9. Outline your lips with a fine brush or a lip pencil which matches your lipstick. Then put on your lipstick. Blot it on a tissue, apply another coat, and blot again.

You could paint your nails with polka dots to match your make-up.

RAZZLE DAZZLE MAKE-UP

You are sure to get noticed in this colourful party make-up. You can vary the colours you use if you like.

YOU WILL NEED:

- Foundation
- Translucent powder
- Orange, sea green and smoky grey eye-shadows
- Black and emerald green mascara
- Orange lipstick and a lip brush
- Matching lip pencil

1. First, smooth foundation all over your face and neck using a cosmetic sponge. You can check the techniques for putting on make-up on page 16.

2. Powder your face lightly all over, using a cotton wool ball or a powder puff. Gently flick off any loose powder with your powder brush.

3. Brush blusher on to your cheeks, as shown. You can put on a little more in the evening than you would during the day, but make sure you blend it in well.

4. Brush orange eye-shadow on the inner half of one lid and the outer half of the other. Then brush green eye-shadow on to the other half of each eyelid. Blend them in well.

5. Dampen a fine tipped brush and use it to stroke grey eye-shadow in a fine line along your upper lash line and at the outer corners of the lower lashes.

An old toothbrush works just as well as an eyebrow brush.

6. Brush two coats of black mascara on to your upper and lower eyelashes. Then brush two coats of emerald green mascara on to the tips of your eyelashes.

7. Brush your eyebrows upwards (you can put a little brown eye-shadow on the brush if you want to darken them). Then smooth them with your finger.

8. Outline your lips with your orange lip pencil (or a lip brush coated with lipstick). Fill in the colour with your orange lipstick and a lip brush, keeping within the outline. Brush a little gold lip gloss on to the middle of your lower lip.

FINISHING TOUCHES

If you have long hair which is not curly, curl it as described on page 53. Tie a brightly coloured scarf around your head in a big floppy bow. If you have a fringe, pull a few wispy strands of it down in front of your eyes and then gently finger a little hair gel through it to separate the curls.

Try to match the bright colours of your make-up to the outfit you wear.

FOUR NOSTALGIC LOOKS

Here you can find out how to create some distinctive make-up looks from the twenties, forties, fifties and sixties. They are not difficult to achieve. The techniques used are the same as the ones you have used earlier in this book.

THE 1920s

In the 1920s girls wore bold eye make-up, bright lipstick and sometimes a false beauty spot. They often wore their hair in a style called a bob.

You will need: pale foundation, translucent powder, black mascara, dark eye-shadow, dark eyebrow pencil, glossy red lipstick and matching lip pencil or lip brush.

Face: put on your foundation and powder, but don't use blusher.

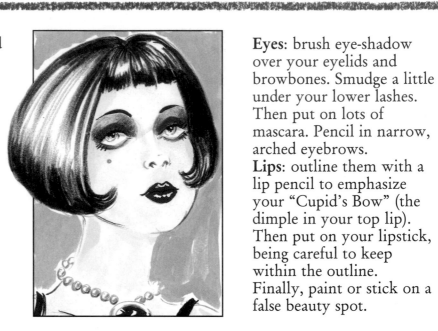

Eyes: brush eye-shadow over your eyelids and browbones. Smudge a little under your lower lashes. Then put on lots of mascara. Pencil in narrow, arched eyebrows.

Lips: outline them with a lip pencil to emphasize your "Cupid's Bow" (the dimple in your top lip). Then put on your lipstick, being careful to keep within the outline. Finally, paint or stick on a false beauty spot.

THE 1940s

Make-up was bold and glamorous in the 1940s. Girls painted on dark eyebrows and bright red lips. They often wore their hair rolled at the front, and left the back loose around their shoulders.

You will need: pale foundation, translucent powder, dark blusher (in brown or plum), brown eye pencil, eyebrow pencil, glossy red lipstick and matching lip pencil.

Face: put on your foundation and powder.

Brush blusher high on your cheekbones.

Eyes: brush eye-shadow on your eyelids, close to your lashes. Put mascara on your top lashes only. Thicken and darken your eyebrows with eyebrow pencil.

Lips: outline them carefully with your lip pencil, squaring off the bottom lip slightly. Then paint them with two or three coats of lipstick, keeping within the outline. Blot your lips between each coat, so your lipstick will stay on longer.

You can try these make-up looks if you have a special party to go to. It is fun to dress the part, too. You could look in a second-hand shop for clothes and jewellery that reflect the same period as your make-up.

THE 1950s

Fifties make-up concentrated on the eyes. Black eyeliner swept up at the corners for a cat-like look. Girls wore their hair in high pony tails, with the front rolled, or worn in a short, neat fringe. **You will need**: light beige foundation, slightly lighter powder, pink blusher, light blue or yellow eye-shadow, liquid eyeliner, a few false eyelashes, eyelash glue, mascara, pink lip pencil and pale pink, pearly lipstick.

Face: put on your foundation, powder and blusher.
Eyes: brush eye-shadow on to your eyelids. Paint a line of liquid eyeliner close to your top lashes, winging it upwards at the outer corners of your eyes. Cut small sections of complete false eyelashes and stick them on at the outer corners of your eyes with eyelash glue. Apply mascara to your upper lashes only.
Lips: outline them with lip pencil and fill in with lipstick.

THE 1960s

Girls in the 1960s wore very dark eye make-up. Faces and lips were as pale as possible. Girls wore their hair in short, boyish hair-cuts, or backcombed into a glamorous "bouffant" style. **You will need**: pale foundation and powder, pale matt eye-shadow (pink or white), grey eye pencil, black liquid eyeliner, false eyelashes, eyelash glue, black eye pencil, black mascara, pale matt lipstick.
Face: put on your foundation and powder.

Eyes: brush on your eye-shadow. Draw a thick line of grey eye pencil along the rim of your socket, and smudge it slightly. Then paint a line of liquid eyeliner along your top lashes. Glue false eyelashes on to your upper eyelids (see how on page 24). Then draw in false eyelashes underneath your eyes with black eye pencil. Put on several coats of mascara.
Lips: cover your lips with foundation, then put on your lipstick.

A GLOSSARY OF MAKE-UP WORDS

On this page, some of the words you will come across when buying beauty products are explained.

AHAs (alphahydroxy acids) – Substances found in natural products, such as fruit. They break down the protein bonds which hold together the dead cells on the skin's surface, revealing newer skin underneath. AHAs are used in many skin creams.

aloe vera – A cactus-type plant. The juice from its leaves is often used in skincare products because of its soothing and moisturising qualities.

anti-oxidants – Substances which fight free radicals (unstable molecules caused by age, pollution, smoking and UV rays). Free radicals can damage skin cells and cause wrinkles. Vitamins A, C and E are anti-oxidants that are often used in skin creams.

collagen – Elastic fibres in the skin which make it strong and supple. Collagen is used in some moisturisers to help soften the fine lines which appear as skin ages.

cruelty-free products – This means that neither a product, nor its ingredients, has been tested on animals in recent years. Most ingredients have been tested on animals at some time in history, but cruelty-free companies do not carry out new tests.

depilation – Removing unwanted hair from the skin.

dermatologically tested – Products that have been tested on the skins of human volunteers to see if they cause itching or redness.

exfoliation – Removing dead skin cells from the surface of the skin to make it smoother and brighter.

fake tanning products – Creams or lotions which artificially darken the skin. There are two main types. Wash-off tans are applied to the body to give instant colour and can be washed off with soap and water. Self tanning lotions take two to three hours to develop after being applied and the results last for two to three days.

henna tattoo (mehndi) – A temporary pattern painted on the skin with a reddish-brown dye, made from the leaves of a henna plant. The pattern fades after several weeks.

humectants – Substances which attract moisture. Humectants are often found in skin creams, as they keep the surface of the skin well hydrated.

hypoallergenic – Products from which the substances that most commonly cause allergic reactions (rashes, itchiness, eczema or puffiness) have been removed. This means they are less likely to cause an allergic reaction.

kohl – A black powder used to outline eyes. Modern eyeliner pencils are sometimes called kohl pencils.

lanolin – A fatty substance extracted from wool that is used in some skin care products.

liposomes – Tiny spheres found in skin creams that are filled with active ingredients. They are so small that they can penetrate the skin and carry the ingredients with them.

lip stain – A lip colour which stains the lips and does not smudge.

perfume – An ingredient used in most beauty products, from eye-shadows to moisturisers, to make them smell nice. However, if you have sensitive skin, look out for fragrence-free brands to prevent allergies and irritations.

pore unclogging strips – Sticky strips of fabric that are pressed on to damp skin, usually the nose, chin or forehead. When peeled off, they remove dirt, dead skin cells and old make-up that can block pores.

SPF (Sun Protection Factor) – A measure of how long a sun cream or moisturiser will protect your skin from sunburn. For instance, SPF 2 lets you stay in the sun twice as long as normal, SPF 10 means you can stay 10 times longer than normal.

sugaring – A method of hair removal. A warm paste made from sugar, lemon and water is smoothed over the skin and allowed to cool. It is then rubbed off the skin or pulled off with strips of fabric.

temporary tattoo – A pattern or picture that is pressed onto the skin, and can be washed off with soap and water.

T-panel or T-zone – A T-shaped area which stretches across the forehead and down the nose to the chin. The oil and sweat glands of the face are concentrated in this area, so it is more likely to be greasy and prone to spots than other parts of the face.

waterproof make-up – Make-up that is resistant to water.

waxing – A method of hair removal. Either warm wax is spread on to the skin and removed with strips, or pre-prepared wax strips are used. The strips are pulled off, taking the hair with them.

Hair

CONTENTS

ALL ABOUT HAIR

Find out how to put rollers in your hair on page 53.

The way your hair looks can make all the difference between going out with confidence or hiding at home. This section will help you make sure your hair always looks healthy and beautifully styled.

There's advice on choosing a hair cut on page 38.

CHOOSING A STYLE

This section of the book helps you to understand why your hair looks the way it does by describing its structure and how it grows. Find out how to choose a hairstyle that suits the shape of your face. There's also a guide to finding a reliable stylist and getting the most from your visit to a salon.

HAIRCARE

You will find out everything you need to know about looking after your hair, from shampooing and conditioning, to creating your own hair treatments from natural ingredients.

THE RIGHT EQUIPMENT

This section includes valuable information on how to choose the best tools to groom and style your hair, and a guide to using them safely and effectively.

PRACTICAL TIPS

There are tips on keeping your hair healthy and shiny with a balanced diet, and advice on protecting your hair all year round.

Techniques such as blow-drying and scrunch drying, plaiting and braiding, and curling your hair are described in straightforward, step-by-step stages.

Find out how to transform your hair for a special occasion by putting it up or adding temporary hair colourants and hair accessories.

HAIR INFORMATION

Charts on pages 60 and 61 will help you decide exactly what type of hair you have, and which hair products will suit you best.

On page 62 you'll find answers to some of the most frequently asked questions about hair, and there's a glossary on page 63 that will help you understand any hair words you might come across.

Find out how to create long-lasting curls in your hair on page 52.

UNDERSTANDING YOUR HAIR

To understand what your hair looks like, it helps to understand how it grows.

A HAIR'S STRUCTURE

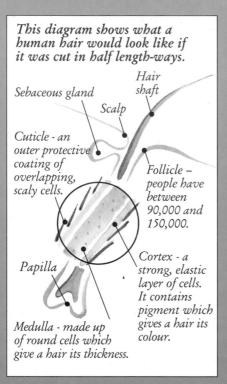

This diagram shows what a human hair would look like if it was cut in half length-ways.

Sebaceous gland

Hair shaft

Scalp

Cuticle - an outer protective coating of overlapping, scaly cells.

Follicle – people have between 90,000 and 150,000.

Papilla

Cortex - a strong, elastic layer of cells. It contains pigment which gives a hair its colour.

Medulla - made up of round cells which give a hair its thickness.

Each hair grows from a hole called a follicle. At the base of a follicle is a clump of cells called the papilla. The cells swell up and turn into hair cells. These then harden and die. As more are formed, the dead cells are squeezed out of the follicle to form the hair shaft.

Inside each follicle is a sebaceous gland. This produces an oily substance, called sebum, that coats your hair and keeps it healthy.

A hair grows about 12mm each month. It lives for between two and six years, after which it dies and falls out. Every day you will lose about 100 hairs, but new ones are constantly growing to replace them.

THICK OR THIN

The size of the follicles in your scalp determines the thickness of each hair. The larger the follicle, the thicker the hair.

Whether your hair is straight, wavy or very curly is determined by the shape of the shaft of your hair and the shape of your follicles. Straight hair has a round shaft and grows from a round follicle. Wavy hair has a round shaft, but it grows from a kidney-shaped follicle. A kidney-shaped follicle and an oval hair shaft produce very curly, black hair.

HEALTHY HAIR

If your hair is healthy, the cells that form the cuticle lie flat. This creates a smooth surface that reflects light well and makes your hair look shiny. When hair is damaged, the cuticles become cracked and frayed. They absorb light, making the hair look dull.

A healthy hair

An unhealthy hair

These strands of hair have been magnified hundreds of times.

A HEALTHY DIET

A well-balanced diet is essential for healthy hair. If your diet lacks certain nutrients your hair will soon begin to look dull and flat.

Make sure your diet includes the following:
* At least eight glasses of water a day.
* Low fat proteins. These are found in fish, seafood, cheese and eggs, nuts and seeds, and white meat such as chicken.
* Vitamins A, B and C. Vitamin A is found in milk, butter, eggs, fresh fruit and vegetables. Whole grain foods, such as oats and wheatgerm, contain vitamin B. Salads, raw vegetables and fresh fruit are high in vitamin C.
* Minerals. Good sources of zinc and iron are liver and vegetables. Milk and cheese contain lots of calcium.

REGULAR EXERCISE

To grow healthily, your hair needs a regular supply of oxygen and nutrients. These are carried to the hair follicles by your blood. To ensure a good supply of blood to your scalp, boost your circulation with exercise.

Seafood contains oils which will make your hair shiny.

Fresh fruit and vegetables are a valuable source of vitamin C.

Wholemeal pasta and bread help your body produce protein to strengthen your hair.

If you eat a healthy diet, you shouldn't need to take vitamin supplements like these.

Your diet should include three portions of vegetables every day.

Try to eat three pieces of fruit a day.

Milk, eggs and cheese, add essential protein to your diet.

Nuts are a good source of oil.

Pulses contain protein which strengthens your hair.

CHOOSING THE RIGHT HAIRSTYLE

The shape of your face is one of the most important things to consider when choosing a new hairstyle. A good cut will emphasise your good points and disguise the bad ones.

YOUR FACE SHAPE

To identify the shape of your face, use a headband to keep your hair off your face.

Stand in front of a well-lit mirror. With an old lipstick, draw around the outline of your face on the mirror. Carefully trace around the shape of your head, your cheeks and your jaw.

Compare the shape of your face with the shapes described in the chart below. The chart will then tell you which styles to choose and which to avoid.

Use an old lipstick to draw around your face on the surface of the mirror.

FACE SHAPE	CONSIDER	AVOID
OVAL Length equal to one and a half times the width at the cheeks	*This is considered the perfect face shape. Almost any hairstyle will flatter it. Straight, sleek styles, short cuts or dramatic swept-back styles will suit you.*	Don't let a stylist talk you into an outrageous haircut. It may suit the shape of your face, but it may not suit your lifestyle.
ROUND Almost as wide as it is long. Full near the cheeks	*Keep the sides of your hair sleek or short to make your face look narrower. Choose styles that brush forward and frame your face to make it look slimmer.*	Resist bubbly curls or full hair. Don't wear your hair swept back off your face. Avoid one-length cuts and hairstyles with a round outline.
LONG Narrow face with a long chin or a high forehead	*Your hair should be no longer than chin length. Curls at the sides of your face will add width. A fringe will make your face look shorter.*	Long, straight, one-length cuts, or hair pulled off your face, will draw attention to your chin and forehead. Don't choose a style without a fringe.
HEART Narrow at the jaw, wide at the forehead and cheeks	*Curls or waves at the level of your jaw will make it appear less narrow. A wispy fringe will make your forehead look narrower.*	A centre parting and a short fringe will make your forehead look broad. Fullness near your cheeks will make your chin look too narrow and pointed.
SQUARE Forehead, jaw and cheeks almost equal in width	*A side parting will make your face look less square. Choose a layered style that falls onto your face. A fringe will soften your hairline.*	Severe, angular haircuts, very short hair or hair pulled back off your face will draw attention to its shape. Avoid a centre parting.

CHOOSING A SALON

The best way to choose a salon is to ask friends whether they would recommend the salons they use. You can tell a lot about a salon from its appearance. Is it clean and tidy? Do you like the decoration? Don't choose anywhere that makes you feel uncomfortable or intimidated. Check that the charge for haircuts is within your price range.

Visit a salon before you make an appointment. Check that it looks clean and hygienic.

A CONSULTATION

A good salon will offer you a free consultation. This is a chance to talk to a stylist and to take a closer look at a salon before you have your hair cut. Talk about how much time you spend styling your hair every day.

Try to have an idea of the style you want. Take along a photograph of a cut you particularly like. Most salons will have style books from which you can get ideas. Some salons may have a computer program called an imaging program which will will combine different hairstyles with a photograph of your face, so you can see whether or not a style will suit you.

An imaging program has created four dramatically different hairstyles for this woman.

LOOKING GOOD

Once you have had your hair cut in a style you like, go back every six to eight weeks for a trim to keep your hair looking its best.

A selection of the tools a stylist may use when cutting your hair.

Sectioning clips are used to clip sections of your hair out of the way.

A single-blade razor is particularly good for cutting short hair and for giving a softer shape to your hair than scissors can.

Electric clippers are used to cut hair close to the scalp.

Thinning scissors have toothed blades. They are used to reduce the thickness of your hair, without changing its length.

Cutting scissors have to be kept very sharp, because blunt blades will cut unevenly.

A stylist uses a comb to separate sections of hair.

SHAMPOOING YOUR HAIR

Shampooing your hair properly will noticeably improve its condition. If you follow the step-by-step guide on page 41, you will stamp out bad habits, such as using too much shampoo or not rinsing your hair adequately.

WHAT IS SHAMPOO?

Shampoo contains detergents which lift dirt and grease away from your hair so they can be rinsed off with water.

WHICH SHAMPOO?

There are shampoos that have been specially formulated for all types of hair, from greasy hair to dry hair, fine hair or curly hair. The charts on pages 60 and 61 will help decide what type of hair you have and which shampoo you should use.

You should shampoo your hair as often as necessary to keep it looking good and feeling clean. If you are using the right shampoo, you can wash your hair every day if you like without damaging it. It is not the frequency of shampooing that can damage hair, it is using a shampoo that contains too much detergent. Harsh shampoos will strip your hair of its natural oils. This may cause the sebaceous glands in your scalp to produce too much sebum to compensate. Your hair will soon begin to look lifeless, dull and greasy.

MAKE A CHANGE

From time to time, vary the shampoo you use, because your hair can become resistant to the ingredients in a particular shampoo.

When shampooing your hair, concentrate on the hair nearest to your scalp. The ends of your hair don't get very greasy.

SHAMPOOING YOUR HAIR PROPERLY

It is important not to use too much shampoo on your hair. Using more shampoo than you need will not make your hair cleaner, and can make your hair look dull. For short hair you'll need a dollop of shampoo the size of a grape. For long hair use a dollop about the size of a walnut shell.

1. Before you start shampooing, brush your hair to loosen any dirt and dead skin cells. Then, lean over a basin or bath and wet your hair thoroughly with warm water.

2. Pour some shampoo into the palm of your hand and dilute it with water. Rub your palms together to work up a lather. Then, using your fingertips, massage the shampoo into your hair.

3. Massage your scalp with small circular motions to stimulate the blood circulation and encourage healthy hair. If your hair is longer than chin-length, don't pile it on top of your head and scrub at it. This will tangle it.

4. To rinse your hair, use a shower attachment or a cup with clean water from the tap. Never rinse with bath water as it contains flakes of skin and soap residue. Only shampoo again if your hair is very dirty.

5. Before you apply conditioner (see page 42), wrap a towel around your head or pat your hair with a towel to soak up any excess moisture. Don't rub your hair dry, as this can tangle it and cause damage.

CONDITIONING YOUR HAIR

Even healthy hair can be damaged by styling with heated appliances, brushing and combing, and extreme weather conditions, so always use a conditioner properly and regularly.

WHAT IS A CONDITIONER?

A conditioner contains substances that will add moisture to your hair and strengthen it. It will also make your hair look more shiny.

Apply a conditioner to towel-dried hair. Wet hair will dilute a conditioner and make it work less effectively.

WHICH CONDITIONER?

Conditioners are available for all hair types in a variety of forms. The charts on pages 60 and 61 will help you choose one to suit your hair.

Conditioning mousse can be left in your hair.

Use intensive conditioners to treat damaged hair.

Light conditioning rinses make normal hair shiny and easy to comb.

Creamy, oil-based conditioners are good for dry hair.

HOW DOES IT WORK?

Shampooing may make the cuticles of your hair ragged. They can interlock with the cuticles of other hairs, causing tangles and knots. A conditioner will coat each hair shaft and smooth down the cuticle, making your hair less likely to tangle. The flattened cuticle will reflect light better, so you hair looks shinier when it is dry.

Follow the manufacturer's instructions about how to apply a conditioner and leave it on your hair for the time recommended. Leaving a conditioner on longer won't necessarily make it work better.

APPLYING A CONDITIONER

1. Apply a conditioner to clean, towel-dried hair. Short hair needs a tablespoonful of conditioner; long hair needs about two. Massage the conditioner into your hair, concentrating on the ends, and distribute it with a comb.

2. Rinse your hair until the water running off it is completely clear. It is very important to rinse thoroughly, as a build up of shampoo and conditioner on your hair can leave it looking dull and lifeless.

3. Pat your hair dry with a towel. Wet hair is fragile and stretches easily, so it is important not to pull or tug it. Comb it through gently with a wide-toothed comb, starting at the ends and working up to the scalp.

HOLIDAY HAIRCARE

Holidays can be a very damaging time for your hair, so you need to take extra care to protect it.

SUMMER HAIRCARE

The sun dries the moisture and oils in your hair, leaving it brittle and lifeless. You can buy gels and sprays containing a sun-screen that will protect your hair. Alternatively, cover your hair with a hat or a scarf. After swimming, rinse your hair to get rid of sea salt or pool chemicals that can spoil your hair's condition.

WINTER HAIRCARE

Cold temperatures, central heating and the wind can leave your hair dry and tangled. Keep it tied back if it is long enough and always wear a hat outdoors. If wearing a hat makes your hair greasier than usual, wash it daily with a mild shampoo.

In damp weather, use gel or hairspray to coat your hair with a thin, protective layer. This will stop moisture in the air from penetrating your hair and making it frizzy.

TREAT YOURSELF

For generations, people have used natural products, such as lemon juice and eggs, on their hair. Here are the recipes for some effective shampoos and conditioners you can mix up yourself. However, make sure you use the treatments immediately, otherwise the ingredients they contain will go bad.

Cider vinegar

Olive oil

Eggs

You'll find ingredients in the kitchen that you can use to improve the condition of your hair.

EGG SHAMPOO

Egg is an excellent cleanser. It clings to dirt and, when you rinse your hair, it drags the dirt away with it. The protein in egg acts as a conditioner.

To make egg shampoo, beat together the white and yolk of an egg in a mixing bowl. Massage the mixture into dry hair and leave it for about five minutes. Rinse your hair thoroughly in cool water.

MAYONNAISE CONDITIONER

Mayonnaise contains eggs, oil and vinegar which will make your hair beautifully shiny and conditioned. You can buy mayonnaise or make your own.

To make mayonnaise, mix a tablespoon of vinegar, and an egg yolk. Stir in eight tablespoons of olive oil. Beat the mixture until it becomes creamy. Smooth it over your hair, and leave it on for five minutes before shampooing it out.

WARM OIL TREATMENT

Treat damaged, dry hair with this warm oil treatment.

Put two tablespoons of olive oil in a cup. Place the cup in a bowl of hot water for a couple of minutes, until the oil has been gently heated. Massage the oil into your hair.

Wrap a piece of clingfilm around your hair, and scrunch it up to seal the ends together. Wrap a towel around your head, and leave the oil on for 30 minutes before shampooing it off. Finally, rinse thoroughly.

QUICK RINSES

Give your freshly washed hair extra body, brightness or shine by applying a rinse. Here are some simple ones you can make:

● **Lemon juice** is particularly good for brightening blonde hair. Add four teaspoons of lemon juice to a litre of cool water and pour it over your hair as a final rinse.

● **Vinegar** gives dark hair extra shine. Add half a cup of vinegar to a litre of water and pour it over your hair. Rinse your hair thoroughly, to make sure it doesn't smell.

INFUSIONS

Some herbs or plants can be used to cure various problems and improve the condition of your hair. Different herbs have different effects, but don't use anything unless you are sure what it is.

To make an effective herbal rinse, known as an infusion, place 25g of your selected herb in a container and pour over 300ml of boiling water. Close the container and leave the herbs to soak in a warm place for several hours. (The longer they soak, the stronger the effect will be.) Finally strain the liquid and pour it over clean, wet hair.

An infusion of sage leaves prevents static electricity from building up in your hair.

Marigold petals will brighten red tones in auburn hair.

An infusion made from nettles will soothe an irritated scalp.

Lavender removes excess oil from your hair and scalp.

Rosemary stimulates hair growth.

An infusion of camomile flowers lightens blond hair and adds shine to dull hair.

BLACK HAIR

Black (Afro-Caribbean) hair is often very dry and fragile. As a result, it needs gentle styling and special care to look its best.

STRAIGHTENING HAIR

A hair straightener or relaxer is a chemical solution. When it is applied to curly hair, it changes the structure of the hair, breaking the bonds that form curls so they can be reformed into a straight pattern.

The process stretches the hair shaft and can cause damage, so always have this done by a professional. Straightening is permanent, and only has to be repeated when new, curly hair grows.

EXTENSIONS

Hair extensions are made of real hair or strands of nylon fibre. They are attached to a person's natural hair using glue or heat to form a seal. They should only be attached by a professional hairdresser.

Extensions come in almost any texture or colour, and are great for adding length and volume to your hair.

BRAIDING

Braiding is a technique in which hair is divided into lots of tiny little plaits which can be arranged in various styles. Braids can be left in place for up to two months.

This girl's hair has been braided and then extensions of long spiral curls have been added.

Braids can be decorated with colourful beads.

Care should be taken when braiding. If your hair is pulled too tight the follicles can be damaged, which may make your hair break or fall out.

CARING FOR BLACK HAIR

Black hair is usually very curly. The curls allow moisture to escape the hair shaft, and they make it difficult for the natural oils to travel down the hair shaft. This makes the hair dry and fragile.

Here are some tips on looking after it:
● Use a gentle shampoo and a rich conditioner when washing your hair.
● Give your hair a moisturising warm oil treatment (see page 44) once a month.
● Regular combing will spread the natural oils through your hair, making it look shinier and healthier.

HAIR ACCESSORIES

Accessories are great for dressing up your hair. You can buy a wide selection from department stores or supermarkets.

Bendies are flexible lengths of wire covered in tubes of fabric. Twist them to secure them in position.

Covered bands will not damage your hair like rubber bands.

Hairpins can be used to secure chignons and buns.

Kirby grips

A zig-zag headband

Hair combs

Claw clips will grip your hair firmly.

Scrunchies are elastic bands covered in tubes of material. They are used to keep ponytails and plaits in place.

Silk flowers attached to a hair comb

Snap hair slides are easy to use.

Slides, also called barrettes, will clip your hair into place. They come in all shapes, colours and sizes.

Diamante slides add sparkle for nights out.

If you wear your hair up, you can dress it up with decorative pins.

BRUSHES AND COMBS

A brush and comb are the basic equipment you need for everyday styling and haircare, so it is important to choose the right tool for the job.

This rubber base can be removed for cleaning.

Styling brushes are probably the most useful brushes. They can be used for blow-drying and grooming.

Many brushes have rubber balls on the tips of the bristles so they do not scratch your scalp.

Grooming brushes have bristles set into a flexible rubber pad which ensures they don't pull your hair.

Radial or circular brushes are round styling brushes. They can be used to create curls or flick up the ends of your hair when you blow-dry it.

A smaller radial brush produces a tighter curl.

BRUSHES

Brushes can have a variety of types of bristles: natural hog bristles, nylon, plastic or metal bristles, or combinations of these types. The bristles are embedded in a handle made of wood, plastic or rubber.

When you buy a brush, choose one with long, widely spaced bristles that will not get tangled in your hair. The smoother and blunter the bristles, the kinder they will be to your hair. Avoid brushes with metal bristles that do not have rubber balls on the tips, as these can scratch your scalp.

To check that the bristles on a brush are not too sharp, press the brush into the palm of your hand. If it hurts your hand, look for a brush with blunter bristles.

Paddle brushes are square in shape and good for grooming long hair.

Vent brushes are good for blow-drying because they have holes, or vents, along the back. These let hot air pass through them. Vent brushes can be flat or round.

COMBS

Make sure you choose a good quality, plastic comb. Look for one with "saw-cut" teeth, which means each tooth is individually cut into the comb. These don't have sharp edges that tear your hair. Cheap plastic combs are made in moulds, and often have rough ridges on the teeth which can damage your hair.

KEEP IT CLEAN

To keep your brushes and combs clean and hygienic wash them every two weeks.
- Use a comb to remove any loose hairs clogging your brush.
- Use an old toothbrush to remove any grease and dirt that builds up on the base of the brush and its bristles.
- Wash brushes and combs in soapy water which contains a drop of antiseptic. Rinse them well, shake off any excess water, and let them dry naturally.
- Check your brushes and combs for signs of wear and tear. Buy new ones if you notice they have rough edges or damaged teeth and bristles.

Wide-toothed combs are ideal for wet hair, which is very fragile. They will not stretch or break your hair.

Use a wide-toothed comb to detangle curly or permed hair.

A mousse comb has two rows of teeth. It is used to distribute styling products evenly through hair.

The tail can be used to create a parting or to separate sections of hair for blow-drying or when using rollers.

A tail comb has fine teeth for grooming hair and a long, pointed tail made of metal or plastic.

This grooming comb has wide teeth for grooming and fine teeth for fine hair.

These fine teeth can be used to smooth any tufts of hair that grow at the hairline.

Afro combs have long, widely-spaced teeth. They are ideal for use on black or permed hair. Some afro combs have a combination of widely spaced teeth and fine teeth.

DRYING YOUR HAIR

You can improve the shape and volume of your hair by using the correct styling products and blow-drying technique.

HAIR DRYER

To dry your hair in a hurry, or style your hair while you dry it, a hair dryer is an essential piece of equipment.

A diffuser spreads out the airflow so hair can be dried more slowly. Ideal for curly hair.

Switch to adjust the temperature

Select a dryer that has adjustable temperature and speed settings like this one.

Switch to adjust the speed

STYLING PRODUCTS

You can use a styling product on your hair before drying, to add volume. Some products will sculpt your hair when it is dry. Follow the instructions on the container. Never use too much of a substance as it can make your hair look dull. Here are some of the products available.

Use clips to separate sections of your hair as you dry it.

A nozzle attachment fits over the end of a dryer to direct the airflow more precisely.

PRODUCT	DESCRIPTION	COMMENT
Setting lotion	*Liquid applied to towel-dried hair before using rollers.*	Helps your hair to hold the curl produced by rollers. Can leave hair a feeling a little hard.
Blow-drying lotion	*Liquid applied to towel-dried hair before blow-drying.*	Protects hair from the heat of a dryer. Similar to setting lotion, but leaves hair feeling softer.
Mousse	*Foam used on wet or dry hair.*	Adds body and texture. Good for scrunch drying (see opposite). Conditioning mousses are best.
Gel	*Transparent jelly or spray applied to dry or damp hair.*	Used to sculpt hair. Wet-look gel will mould your hair into dramatic positions. Messy to apply.
Hairspray or **fixing spray**	*Fine, quick drying varnish that holds styled hair in place.*	Comes in a variety of "holds" (how stiffly the hair is held). Dries hair if left in too long.
Waxes, creams and **pomades**	*These come in different forms, but all are applied to dry hair.*	Will make curly hair less frizzy and give straight hair a more tousled look.
Glosses, serums or **shine sprays**	*Fine liquids that coat the cuticle of your hair with oil or silicone.*	Make hair look healthy and shiny. Particularly good on black hair and for sleek, smooth styles.

A GUIDE TO PERFECT BLOW-DRYING .

If you want to blow-dry straight or wavy hair into a smooth, sleek shape, follow the step-by-step guide below.

Don't start with dripping wet hair. Dry it with a towel or give it a blast of warm air with your dryer to remove excess moisture. Spread a little styling product through your hair to protect it from the heat of the dryer.

Clip the hair you are not working on out of the way.

Hold the dryer about 10cm from your hair.

Keep the dryer moving so it doesn't scorch your hair.

1. Blow-dry small sections of your hair at a time. Starting at the back of your head, dry the lower layers first. Work your way round to the sides and finish with the top of your hair and fringe.

2. To dry each section, place a brush at the roots of your hair, and pull it through to the ends. Point the airflow from the dryer down the hair shaft. This will make the cuticle lie flat, so your hair looks shiny.

3. Curve the ends of your hair around your brush to give them a little curl. A final blast of cold air will help your hair hold its shape.

SCRUNCH DRYING

Scrunch drying will maximize the curl in curly or wavy hair.

First, apply plenty of mousse to freshly washed, towel-dried hair. Tip your head forwards and blow the roots of your hair with a dryer. This will help to create volume. Then, keeping your head tipped forwards, squeeze handfuls of your hair in your fist as you dry it.

Don't brush your hair after drying – this will pull out the curls you have created.

This girl is scrunch drying her hair.

You can use a styling product, called a curl revitalizer, to increase the curl in your hair.

Attach a diffuser to your dryer. This will allow warm air to dry your hair without blowing out the curls.

CREATING CURLS

Whether you want to create tight curls or just add waves to make your hair look thicker, the basic tools and techniques you will need are the same.

HOT CURLS

The heat produced by heated appliances will curl your hair quickly and effectively. There are a wide range of different tools available. Some of the main tools are shown above.

Curling tongs will boost the volume of fine hair. Wind your hair around the barrel of the tongs.

Use heated brushes to smooth hair or to curl it. Keep the brush wound into your hair for 5 seconds.

A crimper and straightener has two reversible metal plates. One side is ridged to give hair a crinkled effect. The other is flat and will smooth curly or frizzy hair.

Heated rollers come in sets which contain different sized rollers for different sized curls. The rollers are heated on metal posts.

CURL WITH CARE

- Before using heated appliances always read the manufacturer's instructions.
- Heated appliances dry and damage your hair, so don't use them as part of your daily styling routine. Always use a styling product to protect your hair from the heat.
- Avoid leaving them in your hair for longer than necessary, as you may scorch it.
- Never use plug-in appliances with wet hands or near water. They can give you a serious electric shock.
- Always unplug or switch off appliances after use.

For curls that keep their shape longer, create the curls with a heated appliance, then allow your hair to cool completely before you brush or comb it through.

USING ROLLERS

Rollers are a good way to add volume to your hair. Follow the steps below to put in heated or cold rollers. To use cold rollers your hair should be slightly damp, and to use heated rollers it should be completely dry.

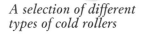

A selection of different types of cold rollers

Wind-in rollers have to be secured with pins.

Bendy foam rollers will produce soft, spiral curls. Wind your hair around a roller and lift the ends up to fix it in position.

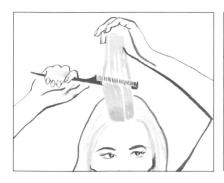

1. Starting at the front of your head, comb a section of hair upwards, away from your scalp. Small sections are easiest to work with.

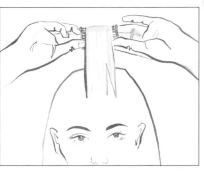

2. Wrap the ends of your hair around the roller neatly. Wind the roller down towards your scalp, taking care not to get it tangled in your hair.

Velcro rollers come in a variety of sizes and shapes. They are easy to use. They grip your hair, so you don't need pins to fix them in place.

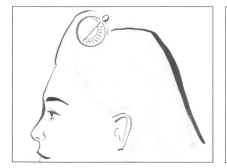

3. To secure a wind-in roller, push a pin through it. Heated rollers have pins or clips to fix them in position. A Velcro roller grips your hair by itself.

4. Repeat the process described in steps 1 to 3 until you have worked your way around your whole head.

Some Velcro rollers are ball-shaped.

TAKING ROLLERS OUT

You should leave heated rollers in your hair for about 20 minutes, until they are cool. Leave cold rollers in until your hair is dry. Finally, remove the rollers and comb your hair through.

A DASH OF COLOUR

Whether you want a hint of colour or rainbow stripes, these pages will tell you all about colouring your hair.

HAIR COLOURANTS

Colourants work by staining the hair shaft (see page 36) with colour. The length of time a colour lasts depends on how far the colourant penetrates into the hair shaft.

When you buy a colourant, there will be information on the packet about what type of colourant it is

Using two or more temporary colours in your hair can produce a dramatic effect.

and how long the colour will last. Follow the manufacturer's instructions carefully. Leave a colourant on for the exact time specified. This will ensure the colour develops properly.

There are three main types: temporary, semi-permanent and permanent.

Temporary colourants coat the surface of your hair shaft with a thin layer of colour. This will be washed away after one or two shampoos. So, if you want to experiment with colouring your hair at home, temporary colourants are the safest to use.

Semi-permanent colourants actually penetrate the outer cuticle of your hair and coat the cortex. They can last for between six and eight shampoos. The colour will fade gradually.

There is also a longer lasting type of semi-permanent colourant.

Temporary and semi-permanent colourants come in many different forms. Here is a selection.

You can add streaks of colour with hair lipsticks.

These penetrate deeper into the cortex of your hair and last for up to 24 washes.

You can use semi-permanent colours to add brighter, richer tones, or to darken your hair. They can only lighten the colour of your hair very slightly.

Permanent colourants contain a chemical, such as hydrogen peroxide, which opens up the hair cuticle and allows a coloured dye to penetrate deep into the cortex. They come in liquids or creams with a separate container of hydrogen peroxide. The two components have to be mixed together before use.

The colour doesn't wash out, it grows out. If you want to keep the colour, you'll have to reapply it to the roots of your hair about every six weeks.

Permanent colourants chemically alter the structure of your hair, which can cause damage. So always have them applied by a professional.

Brush hair mascara through your hair with the wand provided.

Add sparkle to your hair with hair glitter.

BLEACHES

Bleaches don't add colour to your hair, they remove it. They contain a chemical, such as hydrogen peroxide, that lightens your hair by removing colour from the cortex. If left on long enough, bleach will turn your hair almost white. For a more natural look, people often add a golden or silver colour to hair that has been bleached.

CHOOSE A COLOUR

To ensure that a colour suits your complexion, select one close to your hair's natural shade. For example, if your have a pale complexion don't use a colourant that is too many shades darker.

Before using a permanent colourant, experiment with a temporary colourant first.

TESTING COLOURANTS

The colour a colourant produces and the length of time it lasts differs from one person's hair to another's. For example, a temporary colour used by someone with bleached hair will be harder to wash out, because bleached hair absorbs colour rapidly.

Always perform the following tests to check that your hair and skin reacts well to a colourant. If you have any doubts consult a hairdresser.

Strand test – To check that your hair reacts well to a colourant and that you like the colour, do a strand test. Pin the top layer of your hair out of the way and apply the colourant to a lock of hair from the lower layers which don't usually show.

Hair mascara looks dramatic and should wash out with just one shampoo.

Leave it on for the time recommended by the manufacturer before rinsing.

Skin test – Dab a little colourant on to the skin on the inside of your elbow. Leave it for a few hours. If your arm begins to itch or turns red, don't use the product.

You can buy semi-permanent colourants in vivid shades as well as natural tones.

Spray-on colours will wash out of your hair easily.

Some shampoos and conditioners contain colourants.

Semi-permanent colourant mousses are easy to use.

Semi-permanent colourants come in creams and liquids.

PARTY STYLES

Whether your hair is long or short, you can transform it for a special occasion. Here are three looks that are quick and easy to create.

Just follow the step-by-step instructions. You can decorate party hair with slides or temporary colourants.

A SPIKY CHIGNON

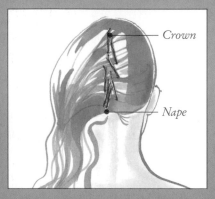

Crown

Nape

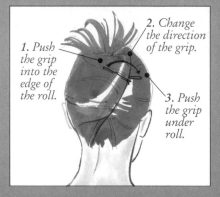

1. Push the grip into the edge of the roll.

2. Change the direction of the grip.

3. Push the grip under roll.

1. Brush one side of your hair back and to the side as shown above. At the centre of the back of your head insert a row of kirby grips, from the nape of your neck to your crown.

2. Gather your hair into a low ponytail. Lift up the ponytail and twist it towards the pins, until it forms a roll at the back of your head. Allow the end of your ponytail to flop forwards.

3. Use kirby grips to secure the roll. Push each grip into the edge of the roll. Then, changing the direction of the grip, catch a piece of the rest of your hair and push the grip under the roll.

MINI TWISTS

1. Divide your hair into neat sections. Twist each section until it begins to twist back on itself.

2. Secure each twist with two kirby grips crossed over each other. Allow the ends of each twist to remain spiky.

3. If your hair is too short at the sides to twist, use gel to smooth it flat. Use hairspray to hold your hair in position.

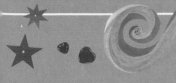

A spiky chignon combines a sophisticated twist with a wild, spiky top.

Spray the spiky top with hairspray to hold it in place.

Add streaks of hair mascara (see page 54) to your mini twists for a really funky party look.

SNAKE TWISTS

1. Brush your hair into a ponytail at the back of your head. Secure it with a covered band.

Two or three matching slides make stylish decorations.

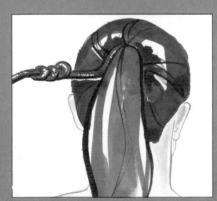

2. Pull small sections of hair free from the outer edge of your ponytail. Twist each section until it begins to twist back on itself.

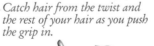

Catch hair from the twist and the rest of your hair as you push the grip in.

3. Using a kirby grip, pin each twist to your hair, above the covered band. You can create as many twists as you like.

With snake twists, you can twist all the hair in your ponytail or just some of it.

57

PLAITING AND BRAIDING

Whether your hair is long, short, straight, wavy or curly, you'll be able to create one of the styles shown on these pages. They are not as hard as they look. A little practice will quickly make you into a fantastic braider.

Decorate your braids with scrunchies and covered bands, or add brightly coloured embroidery threads in contrasting colours.

A FRENCH PLAIT

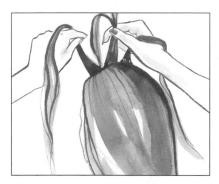

1. Take a section of your hair from the front of your head and divide it into three parts.

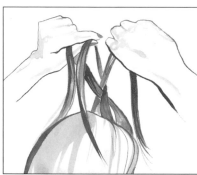

2. Plait your hair once, by taking the right section over the middle one and the left over the middle section.

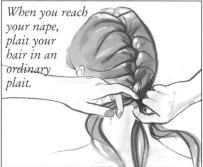

Blend the new hair with the section.

3. Gather up a thin strand of the loose hair next to the right section and one next to the left section. Join the new strands in neatly with each section and plait them once.

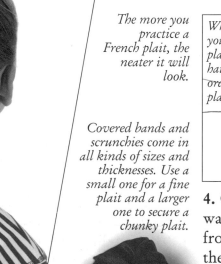

The more you practice a French plait, the neater it will look.

Covered bands and scrunchies come in all kinds of sizes and thicknesses. Use a small one for a fine plait and a larger one to secure a chunky plait.

When you reach your nape, plait your hair in an ordinary plait.

4. Continue plaiting in this way, taking a strand of hair from each side to join in with the plait. At the end, secure the plait with a covered band.

HIPPIE BRAID

For a three-colour hippie braid, you need three pieces of embroidery thread that are about two and a half times longer than your hair. Tie them together with a knot at one end.

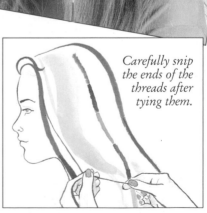

This braid has been bound with three colours of thread.

Tie a knot at the ends of your embroidery threads.

1. Separate a section of hair near the front of the head. Loop the knotted end of the thread around the section and tie the thread securely in a knot around the hair.

You could put several hippie braids in your hair at once.

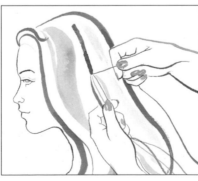

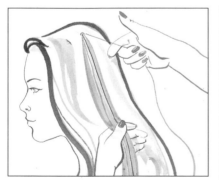

2. Lay two of the threads along the section of hair, and start to wind the third one neatly around both the hair and the threads.

3. After binding about 5cm, swap the threads over, so you are binding with one of the threads which was lying along the hair.

Carefully snip the ends of the threads after tying them.

4. Keep on swapping the threads all the way down to create bold stripes. Then secure the ends by tying them in a small, neat knot.

HAIR TYPES AND TREATMENTS

The sebaceous glands in your hair follicles produce oil to keep your hair healthy. If they produce too much, or too little oil, your hair may become greasy or dry.

The chart below will help you identify what type of hair you have. It will help you understand the condition of your hair and provides tips on how to look after it.

HAIR TYPE	SYMPTOMS	CAUSE	TREATMENT
Normal hair	*Normal hair is usually healthy, shiny and easy to manage. It feels soft and smooth to the touch.*	Your sebaceous glands naturally produce the correct amount of oil. This is helped by a balanced diet and plenty of exercise.	*Use a mild shampoo and a light conditioner. If your hair begins to appear damaged, give it a warm oil conditioning treatment (see page 44).*
Greasy hair	*Greasy hair looks flat and oily. It returns to this state soon after washing.*	Your sebaceous glands produce too much oil. Hair can be made greasy by running your fingers through it, too much brushing, and eating an unbalanced diet.	*Use a shampoo for greasy hair, with a high proportion of detergent to strip the scalp of grease. Apply light conditioner to ends only. Drink plenty of water.*
Dry hair	*Dry hair looks dull. It feels rough and is hard to brush. It is usually brittle, and tangles or breaks easily.*	Your sebaceous glands don't produce enough oil. Hair can also become dry as a result of bleaching, perming, heat styling or the effects of the sun.	*Use a shampoo for dry hair which has added moisturiser. Condition after every wash. Allow hair to dry naturally. Apply a warm oil treatment once a week.*
Combination hair	*If your hair is greasy at the roots and dry at the ends, it is called combination hair.*	Combination hair can be the result of colouring and bleaching, or using heated appliances which dry out the ends of the hair. Very long hair is often combination hair.	*Use a mild shampoo, concentrating on the roots of your hair. Apply conditioner to the ends only. You can buy products specially formulated for combination hair.*
Chemically-treated hair	*Hair treated with chemicals becomes dry, brittle and more difficult to manage than untreated hair.*	The chemicals used to colour and perm hair can damage the cuticle. If you use further chemicals, the damaged hair absorbs them more, causing further damage.	*Colour care shampoos and conditioners help prevent colour fading, and products for permed hair help to maintain chemical balance of the hair.*

SHAMPOOS AND CONDITIONERS

A selection of the different types of shampoos available.

TYPE	PROPERTIES	COMMENTS
pH balance	*Usually has a pH factor (see page 63) similar to that of your skin and hair, which have a pH of between 4.5 and 5.5.*	Useful for permed or coloured hair, to counteract the effects of chemicals on your hair and scalp.
Two-in-one	*Contains detergent to clean your hair and droplets of conditioner that are released to moisturise hair.*	Gives quick results because you can shampoo and condition your hair at the same time.
Herbal	*Contains extracts of various herbs and plants and is available for all hair types from dry to greasy.*	There are specific herbs you can use that benefit each type of hair.
Dry	*A shampoo in powder form which absorbs oil and dirt when brushed through dry hair.*	It takes time to remove all traces of the powder. Can leave your hair looking dull and powdery.
Anti-dandruff	*Contains chemicals that slow down the cell multiplication that causes dandruff (see page 62).*	This shampoo can dry out your hair. Use it once a week, alternating with an ordinary shampoo.
Medicated	*Contains antiseptic to kill bacteria which live on the scalp.*	Not effective on dandruff or head lice.
Insecticidal	*Contains the chemical malathion or carbaryl. These kill head lice (see page 63).*	Very harsh. Use conditioner after each treatment. You can buy special combs which remove lice eggs from your hair.

Here are some of the types of conditioners you will come across.

TYPE	PROPERTIES	COMMENTS
Rinse-out	*Creams and balsams applied after shampoo and rinsed out with water.*	Available for all types of hair, from greasy to dry.
Leave-in	*Sprays, liquids or mousses, which don't have to be rinsed out of your hair.*	Form a barrier around hair which reduces damage from heat appliances.
Hot oils	*Olive or almond oil coats the hair shaft, repairing damaged cuticles.*	Particularly good for very dry, damaged hair. To apply see page 44.
Restructurants	*Penetrate the hair and help strengthen the inner layer of the hair shaft.*	Particularly good for flat hair that is very damaged and has lost its elasticity.
Henna wax	*Thick, clear wax which leaves all types of hair shiny and manageable.*	Has an intensive moisturising effect on dry and damaged hair.

QUESTIONS AND ANSWERS

Here are some questions that are commonly asked about hair:

? How can I add body to my hair?
Choose shampoos and conditioners that contain substances, known as thickeners, that will coat your hair. Only use a conditioner at the ends of your hair. If you over apply conditioner, it will weigh down your hair and make it look limp and flat.

You can use a styling product to give your hair more body. Concentrate the product at the roots. If you are blow-drying your hair, lean forwards and blast your roots with warm air. This will add extra bounce.

A layered hair cut will add volume to even the straightest hair.

? What is dandruff?
Dandruff is a condition which occurs when the skin cells of your scalp multiply too quickly. Dead cells build up and form clumps, which are stuck together with sebum. These white flakes lie close to the roots of your hair. Dandruff is often caused by stress and poor diet. Use an anti-dandruff shampoo and resist the temptation to scratch your scalp.

? Why does my hair break off?
Sometimes hair breaks off in clumps, leaving patches of tufty, short hair. The most common cause of this is using harsh chemicals on your hair, overusing heated appliances, brushing too vigorously, pulling your hair into tight styles, or using rubber bands. Always use fabric-covered bands, and never rub or tug at your hair.

? How do I stop my hair frizzing?
Frizzy hair is often dry, dull and hard to control. Hair can become frizzy if there is any moisture in the air. To avoid frizzing, use a gel when your hair is wet or a serum on dry hair to protect it. These will seal your hair and reduce the amount of moisture it absorbs from the air around you. Use a diffuser (see page 50) attached to your hair dryer to ensure that your hair dries slowly and is not blown into a frizz.

? Will cutting my hair make it grow faster and thicker?
No. Cutting your hair will not stimulate growth. When you have your hair cut, it may look a little thicker because any ends that have become ragged or broken are trimmed off.

? Can I buy a conditioner that will mend my split ends?
No. Split ends occur when a hair shaft splits in two because the hair is damaged. A conditioner will coat the hair shaft, temporarily sealing the ends. However, you can't mend ends once they are split. The only way to cure split ends is to have them cut off, so have your hair trimmed regularly.

? Is brushing bad for my hair?
No. Brushing distributes the natural oils along the hair shaft, conditioning your hair. However, make sure you brush your hair gently and that you use a good quality hair brush (see page 48) to avoid damaging your hair.

A GLOSSARY OF HAIR WORDS

On this page, some of the hair words you might come across are explained.

anagen - The phase of new growth in the life of a strand of hair. It lasts between two and six years.

bob – A popular, one-length hairstyle. This means that if an imaginary horizontal line was drawn around the bottom of the hair all the ends would touch it. Bobs come with or without fringes.

catagen – The period of change in the life of a hair when the sebaceous gland becomes less active and it gradually stops growing. The phase lasts about a month.

ceramide – An ingredient in many hair products which coats the cuticle of a hair, adding moisture and thickness.

dandruff – A condition in which skin cells in the scalp multiply too quickly.

head lice – Tiny lice that breed and lay eggs in hair. They cause an itchy scalp. They are caught by contact with another afflicted person. Lice breed in clean hair. Anyone can become infected, so there is no need to feel embarrassed.

highlights – A technique in which fine sections of hair are lightened with bleach to produce a natural, sun-lightened look.

keratin – The substance from which hair is built.

lighteners – Rinses or sprays which contain hydrogen peroxide. They act in the same way as bleaches (see page 55), removing colour from the cortex of the hair shaft. They are usually applied to dry or damp hair and activated by heat from a hair dryer or the sun. They can be very damaging to hair.

lowlights – A technique in which a colour that is different from the hair's natural shade is applied to small sections of the hair.

panthenol (also known as **pro-vitamin B5**) – A chemical which can make hair look thicker by adding moisture.

perming – A method of using chemicals to curl hair permanently. The hair is wrapped around rollers and a chemical solution applied to it. The chemicals break the bonds between the molecules in the hair shaft. The bonds are then reformed into the curly shape created by the rollers.

pH factor – A number used to indicate how much hydrogen a solution contains. It tells you whether the substance is alkaline or acid. The more hydrogen there is in a substance, the more alkaline it is. Skin and hair have an hydrogen content of between pH4.5 and 5.5. Products with a similar pH are best for your hair.

porous – When a hair's cuticle becomes rough or damaged, it is described as porous.

silicone – A substance that coats the hair shaft and adds extra gloss.

telogen – The phase in the life of a strand of hair during which the sebaceous gland stops working, the follicle shrinks and the hair eventually falls out. This period lasts approximately 100 days.

trichologist – A specialist who diagnoses and deals with hair and scalp problems.

CUTTING TECHNIQUES

Some of the main cutting techniques are described below.

blunt cutting – The ends of the hair are cut straight across. It is ideal for fine hair, making it look fuller and thicker. Blunt cuts are usually one length.

feathering or **slide cutting** – The stylist slides the scissors up and down small sections of hair. This makes the sections of hair thinner towards the ends.

graduating – The ends of the hair are cut at an angle to the head. The hair on top looks thicker and blends with shorter hair at the back and sides.

layering – The hair is cut to different lengths. Usually the top layers are the shortest. Layering gives a rounder, softer appearance to a hairstyle.

thinning – Special thinning scissors or a razor are used to reduce the thickness or bulk of hair without changing its actual length.

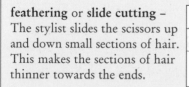

INDEX

ACKNOWLEDGMENTS

Models: Mickey at Synchro, Akure at Look, Emma Campbell and Louise Kelly at Select, Hayley Biggs, Rosie Dickins, Lulu Tabbarah-Nana, Abi Taylor, Rachael Taylor, Amy Treppass, Hanna Watts, and Zoë Wray

Session co-ordinator: Saskia Sarginson and Kathy Ward
Stylist: Sara Sarre
Make-up and hair: Louise Constad
Hair: (pages 14-15, 17, 19, 27) – Tony Collins for Joshua Galvin

The following companies kindly contributed make-up for the photographs in this book:
Ruby Hammer Professional Make-up Brushes; 17, Natural Collection, no.7 all available exclusively at Boots; Rimmel Cosmetics; Sensiq; Revlon International; Bourgois Cosmetics; Flori Roberts

The following companies kindly contributed hair products and equipment for the photographs in this book:
17, Natural Collection, no.7 all available exclusively at Boots, Aveda, Babyliss, Belson Products, Comare, Comby, Denman, Fransen, Jerome Russell Cosmetics Ltd, Superdrug, VO5, Wahl, Wella, Charles Worthington

Special thanks to: Sally Hair and Beauty Supplies for hair products and equipment, and Head Gardener for hair accesssories

The following companies kindly contributed clothes and accessories for the photographs in this book:
Liberty, Goldie, Fenwicks, Corocraft, Katharine Glazier and Extras (both at Hyper Hyper), Alexis Lahellec, Oui, Hyper Hyper, Molton Brown. All room sets from Habitat.

The following organizations gave permission to reproduce the photographs:
cover: Florian Franke/Superstock; pages 10 and 11: Fair skin/brown hair – Howard Daniels/Robert Harding; Fair skin/blonde hair – David Oldfield/Robert Harding; Freckled skin/red hair – Steve Cartwright/ Robert Harding; Black skin/dark hair – Jutta Klee/Robert Harding; Olive skin/dark hair – Oliver Pearce/Robert Harding; Brown skin/dark hair – Adrian Green/ Robert Harding; page 36: Redkin and Dr Jeremy Burgess/ Science Photo Library; page 39: Tom Lee/Worthington salon – Covent Garden, London, UK; Wig Out – Connectix Corp., 2955 Campus Drive, San Mateo, CA 94403

Cover design: Neil Francis
With thanks to: Fiona Watt